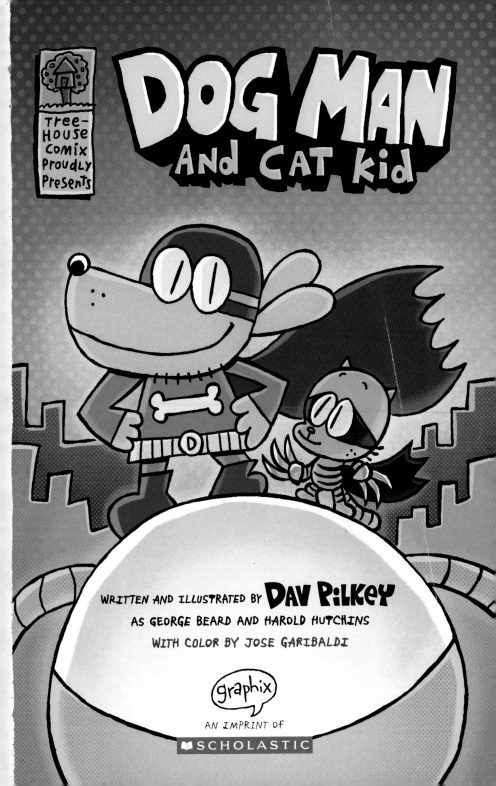

FOR A REAL HERO,
BILLY DIMICHELE

With thanks to John Steinbeck, whose novels, particularly
<u>East of Eden</u>, still resonate with readers today.

Library of Congress Control Number 2017939754

978-0-545-93518-0 (POB)
978-1-338-23037-6 (Library)

10 9 8 7 6 5 4   18 19 20 21 22

Printed in China   62
First edition, January 2018

Edited by Anamika Bhatnagar
Book design by Dav Pilkey and Phil Falco
Color by Jose Garibaldi
Creative Director: David Saylor

CHAPTERS

CHAPTER 2

HOLLYWOOD HERO

by George and Harold

* Italian for "hello." (Pronounced "chow.")

** Translation: Hello, handsome!

Remember,

while you are flipping,
be sure you can see
the image on page 43
AND the image on page 45.

If you flip quickly,
the two pictures will
start to look like
one **Animated** cartoon!

Don't forget to
add your own
sound-effects!

Left
hand here.

Right
Thumb
here.

56

Left
hand here.

Right
Thumb
here.

83

Right
Thumb
here.

CUT!

89

93

94

98

108

123

zeeez

Left hand here.

Right
Thumb
here.

161

Left hand here.

Right
Thumb
here.

172

TRIPLE
FLIP·O·
RAMA

Left
hand here.

Right
Thumb
here.

202

246

252

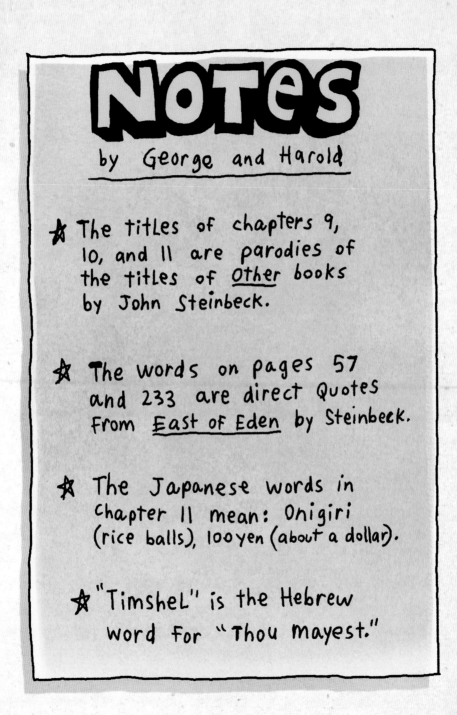

NOTES

by George and Harold

★ The titles of chapters 9, 10, and 11 are parodies of the titles of <u>Other</u> books by John Steinbeck.

★ The words on pages 57 and 233 are direct Quotes From <u>East of Eden</u> by Steinbeck.

★ The Japanese words in chapter 11 mean: Onigiri (rice balls), 100 yen (about a dollar).

★ "Timshel" is the Hebrew word for "Thou mayest."

ABOUT THE AUTHOR-ILLUSTRATOR

When Dav Pilkey was a kid, he suffered from ADHD, dyslexia, and behavioral problems. Dav was so disruptive in class that his teachers made him sit out in the hall every day. Luckily, Dav loved to draw and make up stories. He spent his time in the hallway creating his own original comic books.

In the second grade, Dav Pilkey created a comic book about a superhero named Captain Underpants. His teacher ripped it up and told him he couldn't spend the rest of his life making silly books.

Fortunately, Dav was not a very good listener.

ABOUT THE COLORIST

Jose Garibaldi grew up on the South Side of Chicago. As a kid, he was a daydreamer and a doodler, and now it's his full-time job to do both. Jose is a professional illustrator, painter, and cartoonist who has created work for Dark Horse Comics, Disney, Nickelodeon, MAD Magazine, and many more. He lives in Los Angeles, California, with his wife and their cats.